Dial Books for Young Readers   New York

Four Hungry Kittens

❖ ❖ ❖

Emily Arnold McCully

Published by Dial Books for Young Readers
A division of Penguin Putnam Inc. 345 Hudson Street, New York, New York 10014
Copyright © 2001 by Emily Arnold McCully. All rights reserved
Designed by Lily Malcom
Printed in Hong Kong on acid-free paper
1 3 5 7 9 10 8 6 4 2

Library of Congress Cataloging-in-Publication Data
McCully, Emily Arnold. Four hungry kittens/Emily Arnold McCully.
p.   cm.
Summary: In this wordless story, four kittens share adventures
while their mother is away hunting for food.
ISBN 0-8037-2505-1 [1. Cats—Fiction. 2. Stories without words.] I. Title.
PZ7.M13913 Fo 2001 {E}—dc21   99-088779

The artwork was rendered in watercolor on Arches paper.

for Paula and Martin
and Nat and Tad

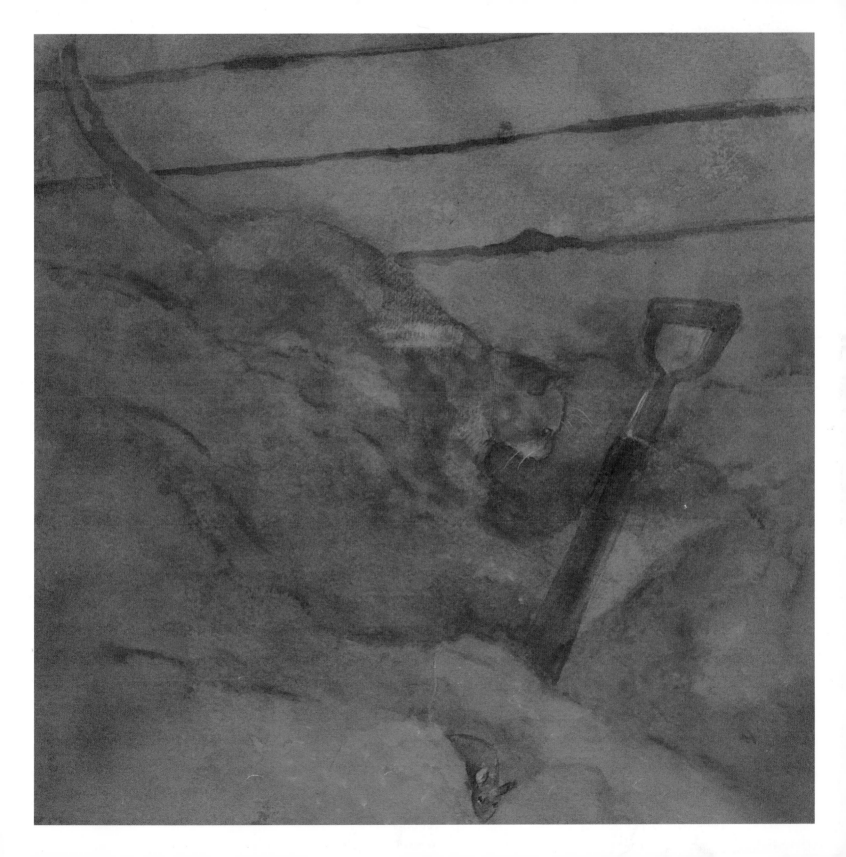